The Adventures of YOUNG STARBURY

PRACTICE MAKES PERFECT

By Stephon Marbury with Marshall Dean

Illustrated by Ryan Nakai

GODSPEED PRESS

I dedicate this book to my wife, Tasha, and my children Stephanie, Xaviera and Stephon II. I also dedicate this book to my family and friends across the world that have inspired it's creation. I hope you will enjoy reading it as much as I enjoyed writing it. The fact that you're even reading this book proves that there is no difference between you and I. We are both trying to find a way to take care of the world's most treasured asset, our children. I thank GOD and you for allowing me to share this book. GOD BLESS!

—Stephon

To my Heavenly Father, I give you eternal praise and thanks. To my parents, Marietta Jones and Harold Dean, I thank you for the gifts of life, love and creativity. To my niece and nephew, Sydney and J.J., my greatest wish for you is that you dare yourself to dream.

—Marshall

To my mom and dad, Barney and Iris Nakai, there are no words that can express how much you mean to me and how you have influenced me in life.

—Ryan

A special thanks to Gus and Aleicia Bass at CAA Management II, Inc., for all your wonderful support and guidance; Marvet Britto for your vital role in inspiring this project; Lonnie White, senior book editor for Rivalry Series, Inc., for all your hard work and dedication on this project and Proofreader, Andrew Lawrence.

GODSPEED PRESS FOR YOUNG READERS

An imprint of Godspeed Press Children's Publishing Division

430 Davis Drive Suite 430, Morrisville, NC 27560

Text copyright © 2007 by Stephon Marbury and Marshall Dean

Illustration copyright © 2007 Marshall Dean

GODSPEED PRESS FOR YOUNG READERS is a trademark of Starbury Trademark, Inc.

Book design by Marshall Dean

The text for this book is set in Garamond

Manufactured in the United States of America

Library of Congress Cataloging-in-Publications Data

Dean, Marshall.

Practice makes perfect / Stephon Marbury and Marshall Dean ; illustrated by Ryan Nakai. Summary: After missing two important free throws, Young Starbury learns that the key to correcting his basketball imperfections is by practicing.

ISBN-13: 978-0-9798250-0-2 (isbn-13)

ISBN-10: 0-9798250-0-8 (isbn-10)

[1.Basketball-Fiction. 2 Self-confidence-Fiction] I.Marbury,Stephon Dean,Marshall II.Nakai,Ryan,ill.IIITitle.

Starbury stood at the free throw line. There were players all around him and the gym was packed with people, but he still felt all alone as he looked up at the goal.

It was the first game of the season and his team only trailed by one point to the Hawks, the best team in the league. Though for Starbury, the game had been awful. More than once he'd lost the ball, made a bad pass or missed crucial shots. But this was his chance to make–up for his bad game.

It was the moment Starbury had always dreamed about. There was no time left in the game and the last two shots belonged to him. If he could just make one free throw the game would be tied, however, if he could make both free throws his team would win.

"You can do it, Starbury!" his family cheered from the stands.

He took a deep breath then tried his best, but he still missed both free throws. His team lost.

After the game, Coach Lou gathered all the players together for a pep talk. "I'm very proud of you, guys. You played your best and you almost beat the #1 team in our first game. I've got a feeling this is going to be a special season for this team."

But Starbury didn't feel very special. He couldn't help feeling that he had let his teammates down and he lowered his head in shame. *If it is a special season, it won't be because of me*, he thought to himself.

Coach Lou saw that Starbury was disappointed, so he tried to cheer him up.

"Keep your chin up, Starbury. One game doesn't prove whether you are a good player or a bad player. It just proves that you've played one game."

Later that night, Starbury sat in his room still feeling down about the game when Eric, his oldest brother, paid him a visit.

"Why the sad face, little brother?" Eric asked.

"Because I played awful today," Starbury answered.

"Don't be so hard on yourself, Starbury. Every player has a bad game once in a while," Eric explained, "Even me."

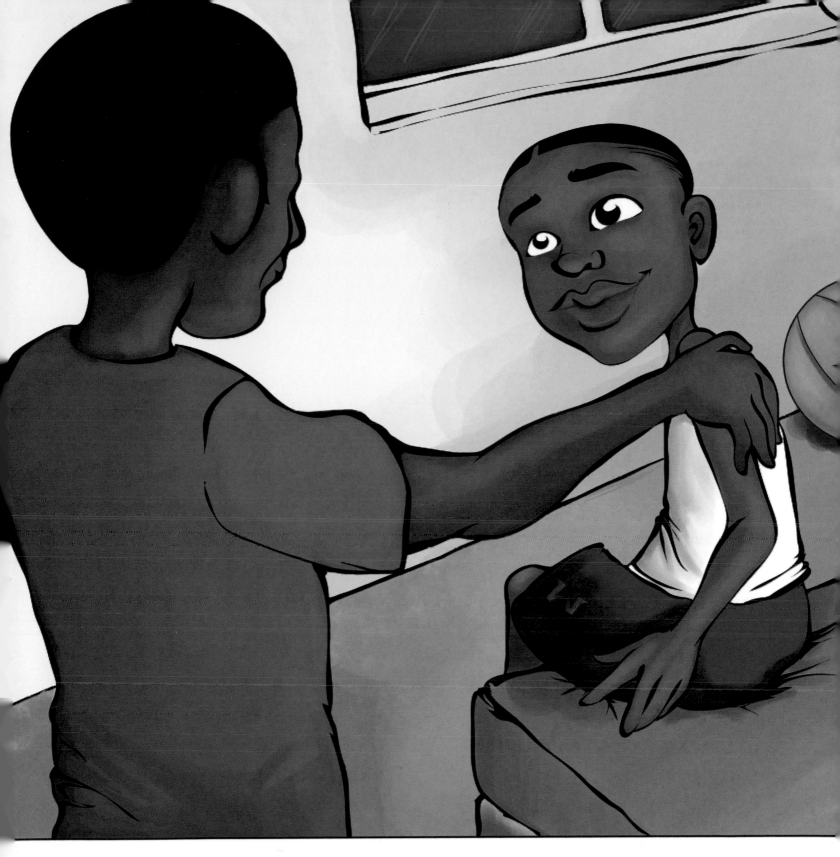

Starbury couldn't believe his ears. His three older brothers—Eric, Don and Norman—all played basketball, but Starbury could not remember ever seeing one of them have a bad game.

"Tell you what, I can't promise that you won't ever have a bad game again, but I can show you a secret that will help you have more good games than bad," said Eric.

"Really? What's the secret?" Starbury eagerly asked.

"Get some sleep. I'll show you tomorrow morning," Eric answered.

The next morning, Starbury bounced with excitement as he and Eric walked to the basketball court. Eric carried a bag over his shoulder and Starbury imagined that Eric's big secret was hidden inside.

At the basketball court, Eric smiled at Starbury. "Are you ready for the secret?"

"Yes," Starbury quickly answered.

"Okay. Close your eyes and stick out your hands," said Eric.

Starbury gladly closed his eyes and stuck out his hands. But he was surprised and confused when he opened his eyes only to discover Eric had placed a basketball in his hands.

"The secret is practice. Practice makes perfect, little brother," said Eric.

Starbury looked down at the ball and thought about his bad game and the two free throws he missed. He promised himself that he would practice very hard to never have another game like his last one.

To improve his dribbling skills, he began to practice dribbling as often as he could and wherever he could. He quickly learned that his dribbling skills were not nearly as good as he once thought because Eric, Don and Norman happily knocked the ball away from him whenever they pleased.

Sometimes, they even playfully stole the ball from him, forcing Starbury to chase them.

Still, Starbury continued to practice dribbling. He even dribbled in his house as he walked from room to room until his mother told him to restrict his dribbling to his bedroom.

In his bedroom, he'd sit at his desk working on his homework with his right hand while he practiced dribbling with his left hand.

As the days passed, he began to carry his basketball with him everywhere he went. He took it school...

Ate lunch with it...

Took a bath with it...

He even slept with it.

To improve his shot, he began practicing his free throws and jump shots. He practiced every day, sometimes several times throughout the day. He practiced in the morning before school... after school... before basketball practice... after basketball practice... and before dinner. He wanted to practice after dinner, but by then it was time for him to do his homework.

He could see that the practice was helping because soon he was making more shots than ever before.

His teammates and Coach Lou also began to notice his improvement in skills. At first they saw it in practice, but as the season continued, they began to see it during the games as well.

Coach Lou's prediction had been correct; this team was turning out to be special. However, Starbury could not have been more wrong about his prediction. In the beginning of the season, Starbury doubted he would have any part in making the team special. But, in truth, his improvement in play was as big a part of the team's success as any of his teammates—if not more.

As the season went on, Starbury continued to practice on his skills whenever and wherever possible. And soon, his brothers found stealing the basketball away from Starbury was not so easy—in fact, it was quite hard.

By the end of the season, Starbury and his teammates were set up for a rematch with the Hawks. But this time, it was for the championship.

On the night before the big game, Starbury visited Eric in his room.
"What's going on, Starbury? Are you ready for the big day tomorrow?" Eric asked with a smile.
"You bet I am," Starbury happily answered.
"Good. Just go out there and do your best," Eric said. "And have confidence in everything that you've practiced."

Starbury nodded at him.

"That's actually the reason I came by, I wanted to say thanks for sharing your secret. Practicing has really helped me," he said.

"Don't mention it. You were the one who did all the hard work. Just remember, have confidence in everything that you've practiced," Eric said with a wink.

The championship game against the Hawks was even better than the first game of the season. The score was almost as close as the first game, 39-36, but once again the Hawks were winning. Starbury had secretly wished all season long for a rematch against the Hawks. Unfortunately he was not having the great game he'd hoped for. He had not lost the ball or had it stolen from him, however, he had missed more than half of his shots. And with each missed shot he grew more nervous about shooting again.

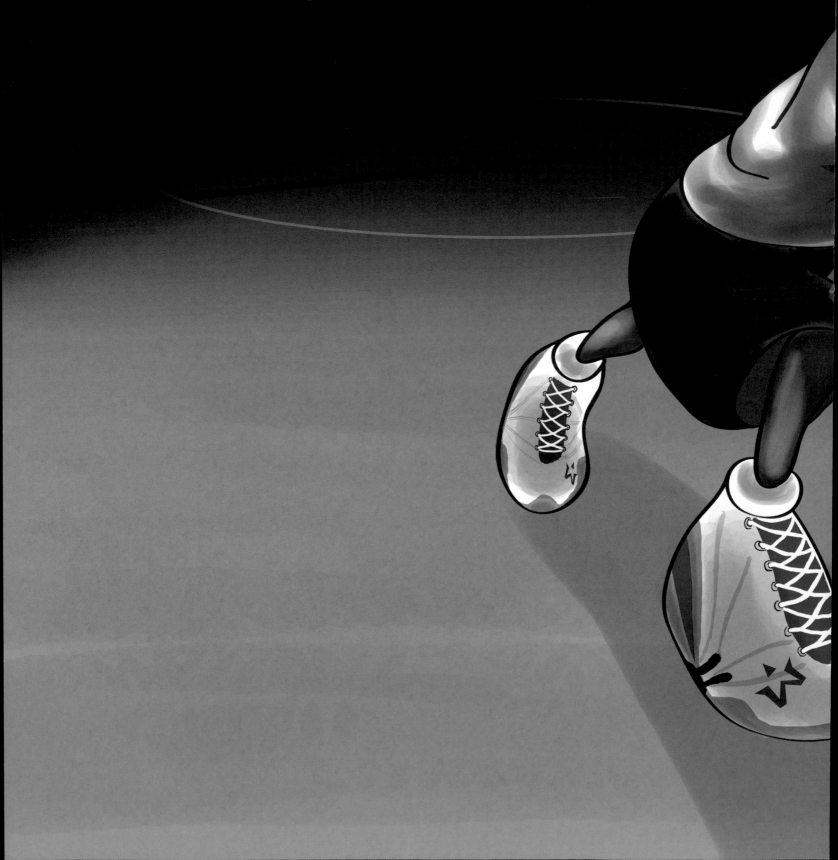

With less than a minute left in the game, a loose ball was knocked toward Starbury. He chased after the ball, but when he caught it he was too nervous to shoot because he'd missed so many shots.

He wanted to pass it to one of his teammates, but they were all guarded. He was the only person open for a shot.

"Shoot it, Starbury!" he heard Coach Lou shout from the bench.

But Starbury didn't want to shoot because he was afraid that he would miss again. Then, all of a sudden, he remembered what Eric told him. *Have confidence in everything that you've practiced.*

Starbury thought about the many jump shots he'd practiced and then he relaxed and shot the ball. **Swoosh!** He made it, nothing but net.

"Yeahhhhh! Great shot, Starbury!" he heard Eric yell from the stands.

However, there was little time to celebrate—his team was still down, 39-38, and there were only fifteen seconds left in the game.

As the time on the clock continued to tick down, the player Starbury was guarding received the ball. Starbury concentrated as he watched the player dribble. And that's when he saw it: the player had the same problem Starbury used to have before he started practicing. He was dribbling the ball too far away from his body.

Starbury knew if he timed it right, he could
steal the ball from the player, just like his brothers
used to steal the ball away from him. So he waited
until just the right moment, then he lunged
for the ball, knocking it away from the
player.

He heard the crowd scream
with excitement as he grabbed the
ball. But before he could make
a play, the player fouled him
just as the buzzer sounded.
The game was
officially over, but
Starbury still had two
free throws to shoot.

Starbury stared up at the goal from the free throw line. He knew he needed to make one free throw in order to tie the game and both free throws to win the championship. Even though he'd practiced very hard on his free throws during the season, he was more nervous now than ever. He tried to calm down by taking a deep breath but that didn't work. The entire season came down to these two shots.

Then as he looked down at the basketball in his hands, he began to smile as he remembered Eric's words. *Have confidence in everything that you've practiced.*

The first shot was nothing but net. The second shot, hit the front of the rim and bounced high into the air. The entire gym held their breath as they waited to see where the ball would land...

And as the ball fell through the net his teammates gathered around him as they celebrated winning the championship.

After the game, Starbury found Eric and they gave each other high–fives.

Starbury smiled at him and said, "You were right, Eric, practice does make perfect."

"Yes it does, little brother. But **shhhh!** Don't tell anyone. It will be our little secret," Eric said with a grin.

Then Eric lifted Starbury onto his shoulders and carried him home.